MUSTANG

MUSTANG

Written by Leslie McGuire

Illustrated by Mitchell Rose

ISBN 1-931020-02-7

Contents

Special Words

Special words help make this story fun.
Your child may need help reading them.

ankle

sugar

1. The New House

It felt as if they had been in the car all day. Montana was a very big state.

"Are we there yet?" Judd asked.

They had just turned off the two lane road onto a dirt road.

"Almost," Mom said. "This is our driveway!"

"Does that mean we can see the house from here?" Grace asked.

"Not for two more miles," Mom said.

Grace and Judd gasped, "You mean our driveway is two miles long?"

Nine-year-old Grace and ten-year-old Judd were on the way to their new house in Montana. Dad liked to study rocks. Mom was a writer.

They had the whole summer until school started.

Soon they came around a turn, and there was the house.

"Wow!" said Judd. "It's a real log cabin!"

"Right," Dad said, "but it's a big one with three bedrooms and a big stone fireplace!"

“Are there any people living near us?” Grace asked.

“Not really,” Mom said. “There’s a ranch over the hill, but that’s about it.”

They had always lived in the city. Grace did not know what it would feel like to be so far away from things. What if they got lonely?

Over the next two days, they fixed up the cabin and got everything put away.

"How peaceful," said Mom. "You can hear the birds singing."

"It's too peaceful," Judd said. "This could get very boring very quickly."

"So let's explore," said Grace.

As they left the house, a light breeze started to blow. That's when an odd sound came from in back of a pile of rocks near the road. It was a thudding sound.

"What's that noise?" Grace asked, but then it stopped.

"Maybe some rocks fell down," said Judd. "Let's see if we can find that stream Dad was talking about."

"He said it was past the little hill over there," said Grace.

It took a while, but they found the stream. It was filled with tiny silver fish.

"Too bad we did not bring fishing poles," Judd said. "I bet there are lots of big fish in this stream, too."

Judd hopped on a few rocks and crossed the stream. "I bet the perfect fishing spot is right over there!" he called as he ran along the bank.

Grace bent down to look into the water. The sun sparkled on the wet rocks. Then she saw what looked like a shadow pass over her head. A soft snuffling sound came from behind her.

Grace quickly turned her head. Standing right behind her was the sweetest little horse she had ever seen. It had a white coat with a black tail and mane. Its big brown eyes had long thick lashes. Its velvety nose twitched.

Grace gasped, and the little horse bolted back into the trees.

2. Who Are You?

Grace could not stop talking about the little horse.

"It's the cutest horse I have ever seen," she said to everyone. "He likes me! I wish he could be mine!"

"That's nice," her Dad said, "but he is not a tame horse, Grace. You just can't go up and get a ride, you know."

But Grace did not care. She carried sugar cubes in her pockets all of the time.

"He was right here by the rock pile," she said. "So I just know he'll come back. I think he's lonely and wants to be my pal."

Over the next two days Grace kept seeing the little horse standing near the house. But he always ran away. After a while, Judd got bored with staying around the cabin.

"Let's go over to the foothills," he said. "Maybe your horse will not be so jumpy out there."

The foothills looked close. They walked for a long time, but they still were not near them.

Suddenly they could hear the pounding of horse's hooves.

"I bet it's my horse!" Grace said.

It was not Grace's little horse that came galloping over the plains. It was a man with jeans and a cowboy hat on a big gray horse.

"Hi, kids," he said as he pulled the horse to a stop. "Who are you?"

"I am Judd, and this is Grace," Judd said. "Who are you?"

"My name is Will," said the man. "You must be the ones living in the cabin now. What are you doing all of the way out here?"

"Exploring the foothills," said Judd.

"Looking for a little white horse," said Grace. "He's wild."

"He must be one of the mustangs," said Will. "There are some herds in these parts, but mustangs are very hard to catch."

"Maybe not," said Grace with a smile.

"Well, it's nice to meet you kids," said Will. "Be careful in the foothills. Watch out for tunnels. There are old silver mines up there."

"Do you mean we could find silver?" asked Judd.

"Maybe," said Will. "Sometimes you see little silver nuggets in the streams."

Then Will rode off.

"It's too late to start looking now," said Judd. "Let's come back tomorrow."

"Maybe we can find silver and my horse," said Grace, feeling very happy.

Judd and Grace skipped all of the way back to the cabin. The sun was low in the sky when they ran up the front steps. They did not see the little white horse that had been following them all of the way back home.

3. We're Rich!

The next morning they set out for the foothills. This time they carried lunch and water in backpacks. Grace had lots of sugar, just in case she saw the little horse.

They walked quickly. Grace looked for the little horse. When they got close to the foothills, Grace saw a flash of white in the trees.

"I bet that's him," she said. "He's lonely and wants to be pals."

"So how come he will not get close to you?" asked Judd.

“He needs to get to know me better,” Grace said. “I just have to wait for him.”

All of a sudden they saw a river at the bottom of a gully.

“Let’s check this out,” Judd said. “This river comes from up the hill. Maybe there is an old mine up there.”

Judd and Grace slid down past bushes and rocks until they were at the river. The water in the stream was flowing fast.

Judd stepped out, using some rocks as footrests. Grace stayed on the riverbank.

Judd bent down to see better.

"I think I see something!" he yelled as he stuck his hand into the water.

But it was just an old pop top from a soft drink can.

Grace walked slowly, checking the riverbank. Something sparkled. She bent down to get a better look.

It was not a pop top. It looked round and lumpy.

Hanging onto a bush, Grace leaned out as far as she could. She stuck her hand in the water and grabbed the shiny lump.

"Judd!" she yelled. "Come and look at this. I bet it's a lump of silver!"

Judd hopped from rock to rock until he was standing on the riverbank.

"Where did you get it?" he asked.

"Right down there," Grace said.
"I bet this is the real thing!" he yelled. "We're rich!"
"Let's keep looking," said Grace.

Just then, there was a crashing sound in the shrubs behind them. The branches were flapping. Twigs were snapping.

"It's my horse!" Grace said softly.

Suddenly a little furry nose poked through the bushes.

4. A Grizzly What?

"That nose does not look like a horse nose to me," Judd said carefully.

The bush flapped and shook. Leaves fell to the ground. Judd and Grace were too scared to do anything but stand very still.

They could hear little snorts. There was a huffing sound.

All of a sudden, there was a loud crack. A little furry ball popped out of the bush. It landed on the ground at their feet.

"It's a baby bear!" gasped Grace.

"Uh-oh!" said Judd. "What if it's a grizzly bear?"

"He's so cute!" said Grace. "Maybe he needs help!"

"Don't go near him," said Judd.

"Why not?" asked Grace. "Do you think he will bite me?"

"Maybe, maybe not," Judd said. "I think the problem is his mama. If her baby is here, then she cannot be far behind. If she thinks you are hurting her baby, she will get really mean!"

"I did not think about that," Grace said, looking around quickly. "What do we do now?"

"I do not know," said Judd. "If we try to run away, we may run right into her."

That's when there was a thumping noise from the trees.

Their heads snapped around. What if it was the big mama grizzly bear?

Grace gasped happily as she saw who had come to see them! It was the little white horse!

"Look!" Grace said."He followed us! He wants to be my pal!"

But the little horse went right up to the baby bear and lowered his head. The bear stopped and looked back. Then the horse began to push the baby bear with his nose!

The bear began to walk. It was trying to get away from the horse. He was going away from Judd and Grace, too. The little horse kept pushing with his nose.

"I think he's trying to make the baby bear go away before the mama comes here," whispered Grace.

Judd just shook his head.

As they watched, the little horse kept nosing the baby bear deeper and deeper into the forest until they could not hear them anymore.

Judd let out a sigh.

"That was close," he said. "Let's get out of here."

5. The Best Pal Ever!

Judd and Grace scrambled back up the gully as fast as they could go.

They had just reached the top when, all of a sudden, Grace tripped on a log.

Grace fell and began to roll down the slope of the gully. In no time at all, she was back at the bottom.

"Ouch!" she yelled.

"Are you hurt?" called Judd as he slid down to her.

"My ankle really hurts," Grace moaned. "What if I broke it?"

"Let me take a look," Judd said.

Grace pulled up the leg of her jeans. Her ankle was starting to turn blue.

"That does not look good," Judd said. "Can you walk on it?"

Grace stood up, but as soon as she put her sore foot down on the ground, tears filled her eyes.

"I can't," she sobbed. "Now what?"

"Just stay here," Judd said, looking up at the top of the gully. "I'll go get help. It will not take long!"

"Hurry," moaned Grace. "I do not like being here by myself."

"Just sit up on this rock. Stay out of sight," said Judd. "I'll be right back!"

As soon as Judd had gone, it got very lonely. Grace's ankle throbbed painfully. She did not like being in the gully. She felt very unsafe. There were bears and who knows what kinds of wild things out here.

"What about snakes?" she said to herself. Anything could happen.

What if Mom and Dad came back when it was dark? What if they could not find the gully again?

Grace could not help it. She started to cry.

Just then, Grace felt a soft warm puff of air at her back. She whipped around with a gasp. What if the big mama bear had come back!

But it was not the bear. It was the little horse!

The horse dipped his head and rubbed his nose on her arm. Then he gave her a little push.

Grace reached into her pocket and gave him a lump of sugar. He ate it happily and pushed her again.

"I can't get up," Grace said softly. Then she lifted her leg. "My ankle hurts too much."

The little horse sniffed at her ankle.

Then he walked around in front of her. He grabbed her shirt in his teeth and pulled up.

"What do you want?" Grace asked softly. Then she got it. "I know! You want me to ride on you!"

With the little horse's help, Grace got up on the rock. She grabbed the little horse's mane. He stood very close so she could swing her leg over his back.

As soon as she was up, the horse snorted. He climbed out of the gully and set off across the grassy plain. He was heading for the cabin.

Grace patted his neck. "I will call you Prince because you saved me!"

Grace and Prince got to the cabin just as Judd, Mom, and Dad were getting into the car. Judd's mouth dropped open, and Dad looked upset. But Mom just smiled.

"Grace was right," Mom said. "That little horse just wanted a pal."

Mom checked Grace's ankle. It was twisted but not broken.

"Wow," Dad said when he checked the lump of silver.

"But Prince is the best!" Grace said, rubbing the horse's neck.

"He's still wild," said Dad.

"Not anymore," said Judd. "He wanted a pal. He was lonely, too!"

"He is the best pal ever," said Grace. "Prince will never be lonely again!"